MW01099115

EXTREME!

Uncovering Mummies
and Other Mysteries of
the Ancient World

Paul Harrison

Capstone press

Fact Finders is published by Capstone Press,
a Capstone Publishers company.
151 Good Counsel Drive, P.O. Box 669,
Mankato, Minnesota 56002.
www.capstonepress.com

First published 2009

Library of Congress Cataloging-in-Publication Data

Harrison, Paul, 1969-
  Uncovering mummies and other mysteries of the
  ancient world / by Paul Harrison.
    p. cm. -- (Fact finders. Extreme adventures!)
  Includes bibliographical references and index.
  Summary: "Discusses the history, making, and discovery
  of mummies from around the world"--Provided by
  publisher.
  ISBN 978-1-4296-4562-1 (library binding)
  ISBN 978-1-4296-4624-6 (pbk.)
1. Mummies--Juvenile literature. 2. Civilization, Ancient--
Miscellanea--Juvenile literature. I. Title.

GN293.H38 2010
393'.3--dc22

2009027856

Produced for A & C Black by
Monkey Puzzle Media Ltd
48 York Avenue
Hove BN3 1PJ, UK

MONKEY PUZZLE MEDIA LTD

Editor: Susie Brooks
Design: Mayer Media Ltd
Picture research: Lynda Lines
Series consultants: Jane Turner and James de Winter

This book is produced using paper that is made from
wood grown in managed, sustainable forests. It is natural,
renewable, and recyclable. The logging and manufacturing
processes conform to the environmental regulations of the
country of origin.

Printed in Malaysia by Tien Wah Press (Pte.) Ltd

102009
005558

Picture acknowledgements
Alamy pp. 18 (North Wind Picture Archives), 26–27
(Dennis Cox); Art Archive p. 26 left (Musée du Louvre,
Paris/Gianni Dagli Orti); Camera Press pp. 15 (Gamma/
Duclos Alexis), 17 (New China News Agency); Corbis
pp. 6 bottom left (Claudio Castellon/epa), 11 (Vienna
Report Agency), 14 (Chris Rainier), 28 (Ryan Pyle/None);
Adam Husted p. 21; iStockphoto p. 4; MPM Images pp.
5 bottom right (Universal Pictures), 12, 16 (Smithsonian
National Museum of Natural History), 24 left (University
College London); National Geographic Society pp. 8 left,
8 right; Rex Features pp. 1 (Sipa Press), 10 (Sipa Press),
19 (Sipa Press), 24–25 (Sipa Press), 29 (Wotjek Laski);
Science Photo Library pp. 9 (Christian Jegou/Publiphoto
Diffusion), 13 (Silkeborg Museum, Denmark/Munoz-Yague),
20 (Alexander Tsiaras), 23 (British Museum/Munoz-Yague);
Topfoto.co.uk p. 22; Werner Forman Archive p. 5 left
(E. Strouhal/Naprstek Muaseum, Prague); Wikimedia
Commons pp. 6–7 (British Museum).

The front cover shows a mummy in the catacombs of
Palermo, Italy (MPM Images).

Every effort has been made to contact copyright holders
of material reproduced in this book. Any omissions will
be rectified in subsequent printings if notice is given to the
publishers.

CONTENTS

What is a mummy?

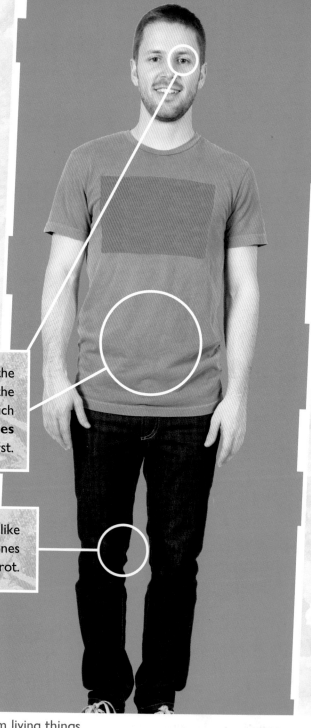

Mummies stumble around, wrapped in bandages, preying on human flesh—at least they do in the movies. Real life is different, but it can be just as gruesome.

Your body is designed to rot, or decompose. When you die, the **bacteria** that have been living quietly inside your body really go to town. They start to eat you—from the inside out!

The rotting process has to be stopped for a body to become a mummy. If a body is mummified, it can last for thousands of years.

A healthy body is full of bacteria—they won't start to eat you until you're dead.

Soft parts of the body such as the eyes, stomach and **intestines** rot away first.

Hard parts like teeth and bones are last to rot.

bacteria tiny cells that can both help and harm living things

4

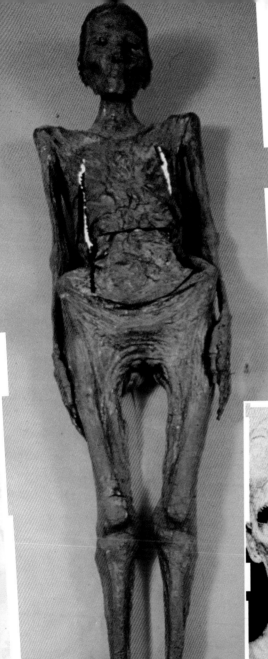

Movie mummies!

In 1932, the horror movie *The Mummy* came out. Boris Karloff played an ancient Egyptian priest who had been brought back to life. Even Boris's own "mummy" wouldn't have recognized him—he was wrapped in bandages! Mummies have been a hit at the movies ever since.

She may not look that healthy, but this mummy is over 1,000 years old.

A poster for the first major mummy movie.

and now **KARLOFF**
THE UNCANNY
as
"The **MUMMY**
It comes to Life!

A UNIVERSAL PICTURE

intestines the tube from your stomach to your bottom

Air dryer

Mummies are sometimes made by accident. If the air is dry enough, bodies dry out instead of rotting— and become mummies.

Watery wonder

Between 55 and 65 percent of an adult human's body is made of water.

This air-dried mummy from China is curled up, just like he was when he died.

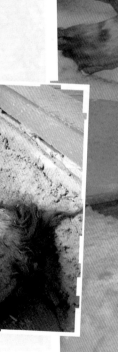

withered dried out   **preserve** to keep, or make last

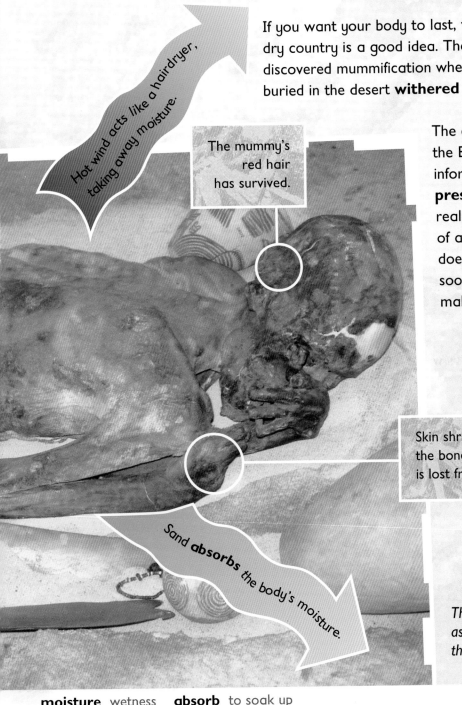

If you want your body to last, then dying in a hot, dry country is a good idea. The ancient Egyptians discovered mummification when they found that bodies buried in the desert **withered** rather than rotted.

The desert mummies gave the Egyptians the basic information about how to **preserve** a body. They realized that if you get rid of a body's **moisture**, it doesn't rot. The Egyptians soon became mummy-making experts.

Hot wind acts like a hairdryer, taking away moisture.

The mummy's red hair has survived.

Skin shrinks tight to the bones as water is lost from the body.

Sand **absorbs** the body's moisture.

This mummy is known as Ginger, thanks to the color of his hair.

moisture wetness   **absorb** to soak up

Making a mummy

What do salt and a long metal hook have in common? Well, they are two of the things that the ancient Egyptians used to make bodies last for thousands of years.

Mummification stage 1: **Organs** *such as the brain, lungs, and liver contain lots of water, so they are removed.*

Large hook pulls the brain out through the nose.

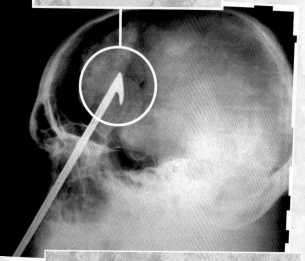

Poor show

Mummification was very expensive, so poor Egyptians had to make do with being buried in the sand.

Stage 2: The body is dried out for 40 days in a salt called natron.

organs parts of the body that do special jobs

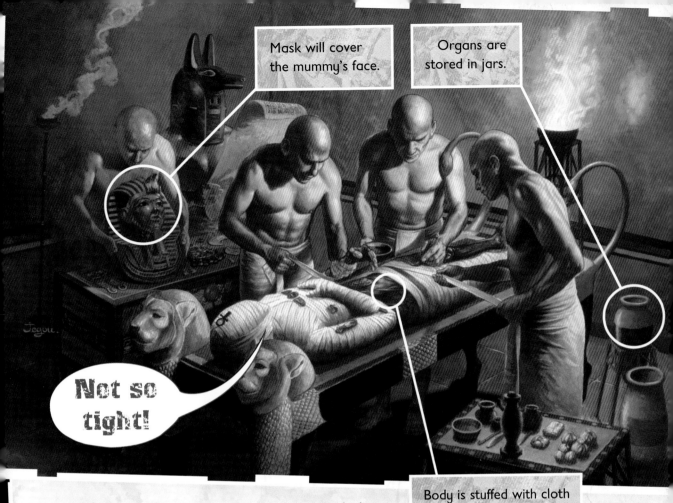

The Egyptians believed that when people died, they went on to an **afterlife**. This made it important for bodies to be preserved. Mummification became a religious ceremony, carried out by priests saying prayers and casting spells.

If the whole point was to make bodies last, then the Egyptians did a great job. They had really worked out the best way of drying a body so that it wouldn't rot.

Stage 3: The body is wrapped in bandages and prepared for burial.

afterlife life after death

Ice man

The weather high up in the mountains is icy cold. It can have the same effect as a giant freezer when it comes to dead bodies—keeping them fresh for ages.

In the past, people from Peru used the cold mountain air to mummify their dead relatives.

When two hikers found the **corpse** of a man in the Alps, they thought it was a recent body. It turned out to be a 5,300-year-old mummy! How and why he died remained a mystery for years. Eventually scientists discovered the end of a **flint** arrow buried in his shoulder, proving that the ice man had been murdered a long time ago.

corpse a dead body   **flint** a type of stone used for old tools and weapons

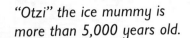
"Otzi" the ice mummy is more than 5,000 years old.

Bodies in the freezer

Some people pay to be frozen when they die, hoping they might be brought back to life in the future! This is called cyronics.

Cold mountain air freezes the body.

Otzi's last meal of meat and bread is still inside his stomach.

Tree **pollen** on the body shows that Otzi died during the spring.

Bacteria don't like the cold, so Otzi's body did not rot.

pollen a powdery substance that plants use to reproduce

11

Bog bodies

Getting trapped in a bog would be bad news—you could get sucked down and drown. On the plus side, your body might become a famous mummy!

*This bog body has been flattened by the heavy **peat**.*

Bog water dyes hair red.

Grisly secrets

Some bodies found in bogs seem to show that they had been killed as a punishment, or even **sacrificed**.

You'd think that a body in a really wet place like a bog would rot quickly—but that's not what happens at all. Instead bodies in bogs get pickled, like dill pickles, before they rot.

There's very little air in bog water, and the bacteria that rot bodies need air to survive. Also, the water is full of plants that make the water slightly **acid**—like the vinegar that cucumbers are pickled in.

peat mixture of rotting plants and water   **sacrificed** killed as part of a religious ceremony

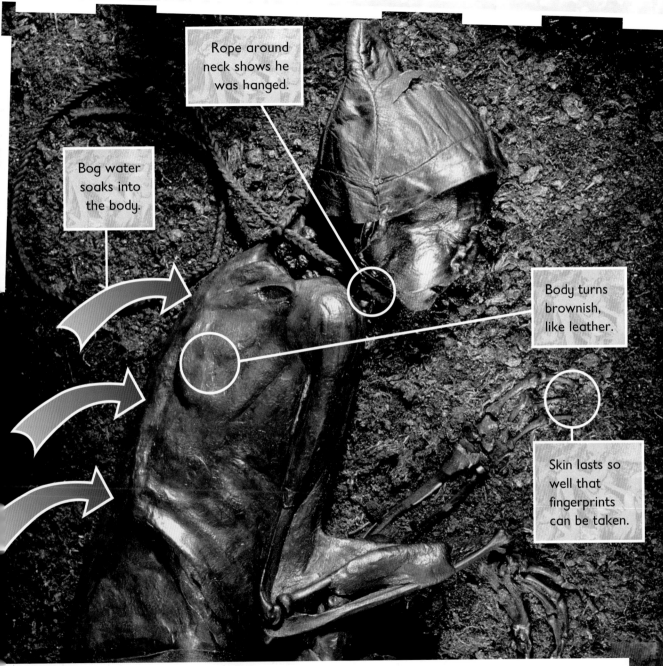

"Tollund Man" lived 6,000 years ago—until he was hanged and buried in a bog.

Rope around neck shows he was hanged.

Bog water soaks into the body.

Body turns brownish, like leather.

Skin lasts so well that fingerprints can be taken.

acid substance that can cause chemical changes

13

Smokin' mummies

Death doesn't always mean saying good-bye forever. Some people mummify relatives so they can still visit them—even though they're no longer alive!

Smoked mummies from Papua New Guinea do a lot of sitting around.

In Papua New Guinea, dead bodies are preserved using smoke—a bit like a butcher smokes ham. The mummies are then displayed in a high place that overlooks the village or are placed in local huts. In this way, the villagers feel that the dead are still part of their **community**.

Bad—and good

Tobacco smoke is bad for your health—but it's great for preserving dead bodies!

community a group of people who live near each other   **dehydrate** to dry out

Tobacco smoke was blown into the corpse to dry the insides.

You might find a mummy like this in the mountains of the Philippines.

Tattooed skin survives.

Person drank a salty drink before death to help **dehydrate** the body.

Body was dried over a fire.

Good as new?

Imagine opening an old coffin and finding a well-preserved body inside! It sounds like a scene from a vampire movie, but it can really happen.

A coffin and where it is buried can have surprising effects on a corpse—especially if an **airtight** coffin is buried in damp, cold ground. In these conditions, the fats inside the body can turn into a waxy or soaplike substance called adipocere. This can make the body look as if it has stopped rotting altogether.

Fangtastic tales

Vampire legends might have their roots in the discovery of well-preserved **adipocere** corpses.

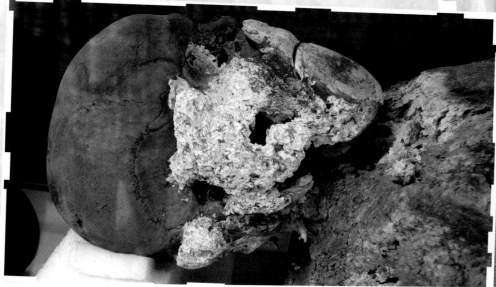

The "Soap Man" is a body preserved by adipocere.

adipocere name given to body fats when they turn soapy or waxy after death

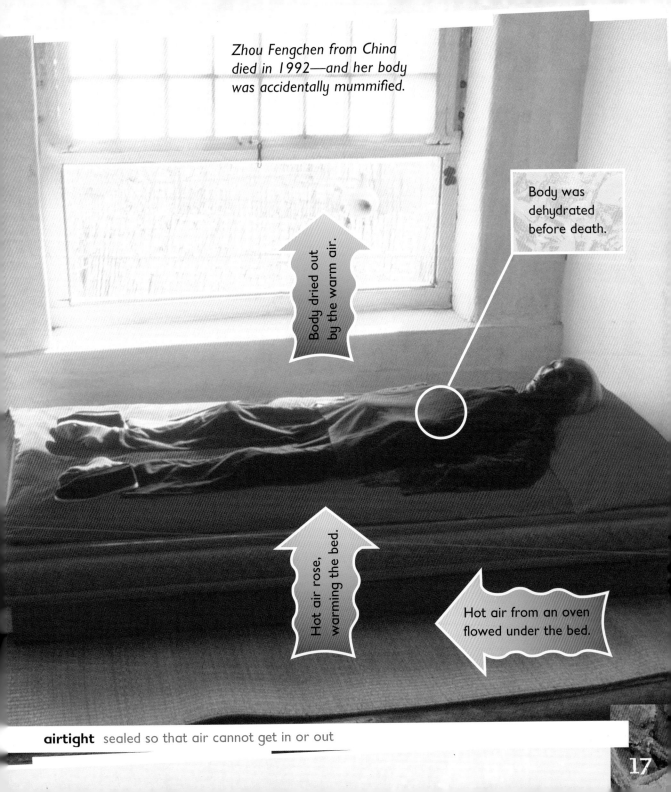

Zhou Fengchen from China died in 1992—and her body was accidentally mummified.

Body dried out by the warm air.

Body was dehydrated before death.

Hot air rose, warming the bed.

Hot air from an oven flowed under the bed.

airtight sealed so that air cannot get in or out

Mummy misery

How would you like to be stuck in a glass case—in the nude—for people to stare at? That's what some mummies have to put up with!

Throughout history, mummies have been treated terribly by people who didn't realize (or didn't care) what they were handling:

- Mummies have been sold by **tomb** robbers to wealthy collectors.
- Some have been ground up and used in medicine.
- In Guanajuato, Mexico, people had to pay to stay buried! If relatives could not afford the fees, then the bodies were dug up and put on display in a museum.

No fuel like an old fuel

As mummies are very dry, it is claimed that some were burned as fuel for steam trains!

Parties to watch a mummy being unwrapped were popular in Victorian Britain.

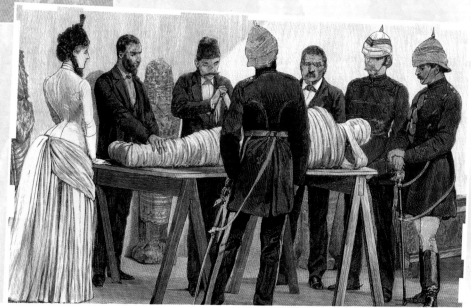

tomb a burial chamber

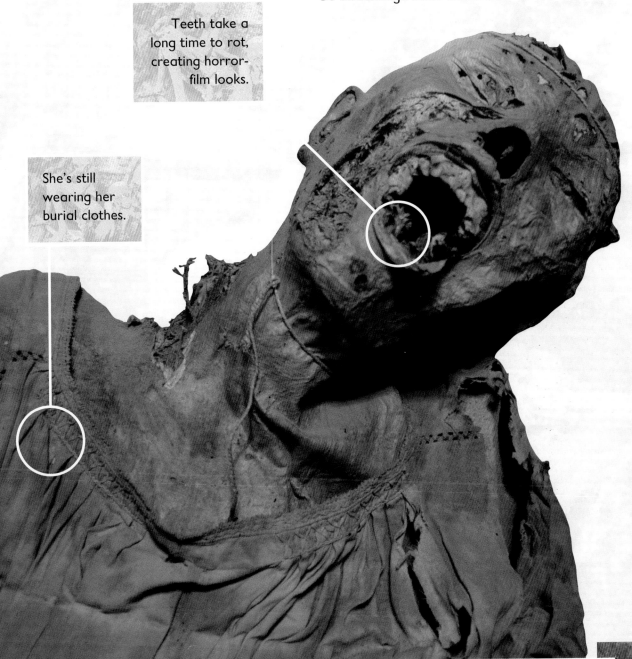

This Mexican mummy from Guanajuato appears to be screaming. Could she have been buried alive?

Teeth take a long time to rot, creating horror-film looks.

She's still wearing her burial clothes.

Under wraps

Taking a mummy to hospital seems a bit odd—after all, it's a bit late for a doctor to do anything. It's not too late for **archaeologists**, though.

Archaeologists use high-tech hospital machinery to look inside mummies—without having to remove any bandages. **X-ray machines** and **CT scanners** beam rays of energy, called X-rays, through the mummy. Hard parts, such as bones, absorb the rays, while soft parts, such as skin, let the rays through. The results are then shown on a photograph.

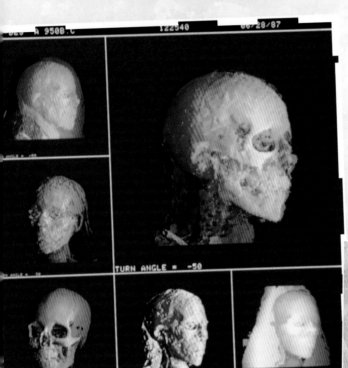

CT scans show the skull of an Egyptian mummy called Ta-bes.

Mystery solved

Many people thought that the ancient Egyptian King Tutankhamun was murdered. In fact, modern investigations found he had died from an infected leg wound.

archaeologist someone who studies ancient peoples by looking at their remains

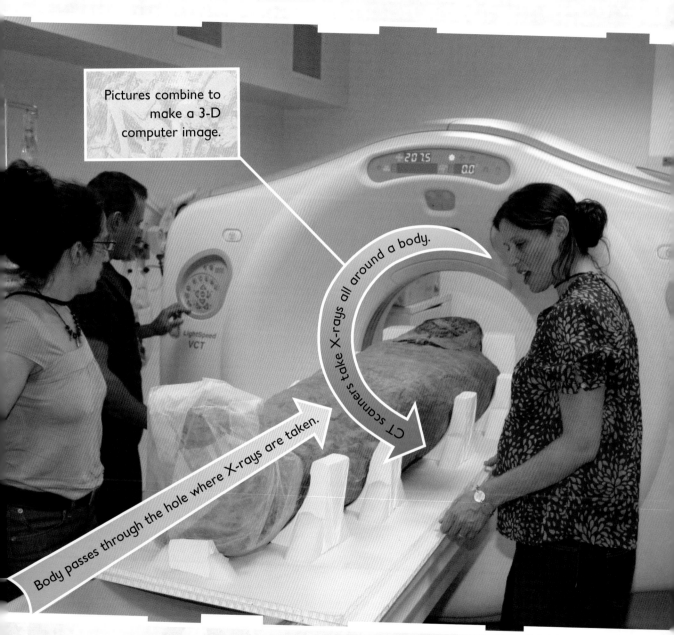

Mummies don't even have to leave their coffins to be scanned.

Pictures combine to make a 3-D computer image.

CT scanners take X-rays all around a body.

Body passes through the hole where X-rays are taken.

X-ray machines and **CT scanners** machines that take pictures of the inside of a body

Back from the dead

Do looks matter? Archaeologists think so, which is why they spend so much time studying mummies to work out what they might have looked like.

Reconstructions have been made from this 2,000 year-old bog body, known as Lindow Man.

1 Skull is usually copied first.

reconstruction a copy of something that no longer survives

22

2 Flesh and muscles are added next, using local people as a guide to facial features.

Reconstructing the faces of people who have died is a skill that the police often use when solving crimes. It's useful for archaeologists, too. They can get a good idea of what a mummy might have looked like when he or she was alive. Sometimes looks can tell them other things about a person, too.

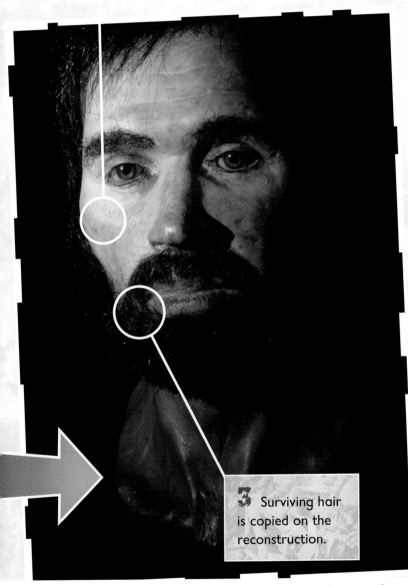

3 Surviving hair is copied on the reconstruction.

Hand history

Archaeologists look at different parts of mummies for clues about their lives. Rough hands or fingernails show that the person probably did **manual work.**

This is what Lindow Man might have looked like in life.

manual work working with your hands, as in farming, for example

Celebrity mummies

Important people—including kings, priests, and even politicians—have been mummified throughout history.

Russian leader Vladimir Lenin's body is on display in Moscow.

Face and hands occasionally show signs of rotting.

My feet smell!

Jeremy Bentham's real head used to sit between the feet of his mummy.

No one really knows why the **philosopher** Jeremy Bentham wanted to be mummified. But we do know that his head fell off in the process, and had to be replaced with a wax one!

The Russian political leader Vladimir Lenin had no idea that he would be mummified. On his death, the government decided to preserve his body so the Russian people could pay their respects.

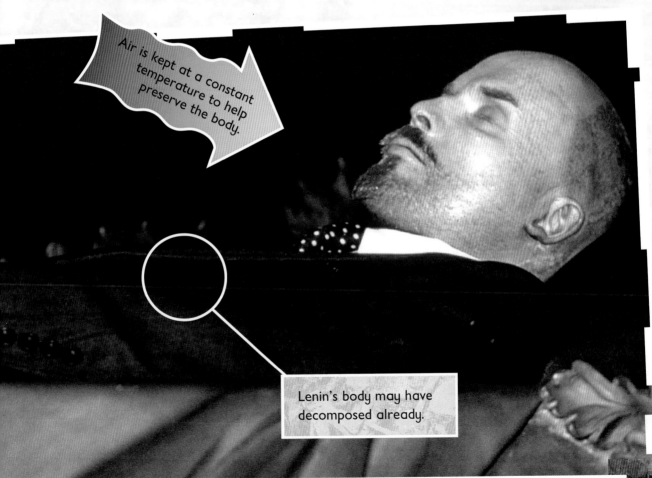

Air is kept at a constant temperature to help preserve the body.

Lenin's body may have decomposed already.

philosopher someone who thinks about and studies life

Fakes and mistakes

When is a mummy not a mummy?
When it's a fake or a mistake! Sometimes
mummies are not what they appear . . .

Occasionally museums have discovered that the
mummies they have on display are actually fakes—
nothing more than bandages stuffed with cloths.
They had been conned!

Not all empty body coverings are fakes, though.
In some cases, real attempts to mummify bodies
have failed—leaving nothing but the clothes or
coffin the body was buried in.

*Faking a
small animal
mummy is
easier than
faking a
human mummy.*

jade a valuable gemstone

*A Chinese emperor once lay inside this head-to-toe **jade** suit.*

Animal antics

The Egyptians mummified animals they thought were **sacred**, such as cats, crocodiles, and even bulls.

Suit is made from jade plates, sewn together with gold thread.

Jade was thought to preserve bodies—but unfortunately it doesn't.

sacred important or holy in a particular religion

27

Modern mummies

Believe it or not, people are still being mummified today—though things have moved on since ancient Egyptian times!

A German professor called Gunther von Hagens has discovered a new way of making mummies. He uses a process called plastination.

A plastinated body gets ready for an exhibition.

Plastination works by **dissolving** all of a body's fat and replacing the body's water with liquid plastic. Once plastinated, the mummies go on display in museums and galleries around the world. Being dead has become a great way of attracting visitors!

Plastic pets

Any living thing can be plastinated, from tiny insects to large animals such as horses.

dissolve to break down a solid in a liquid

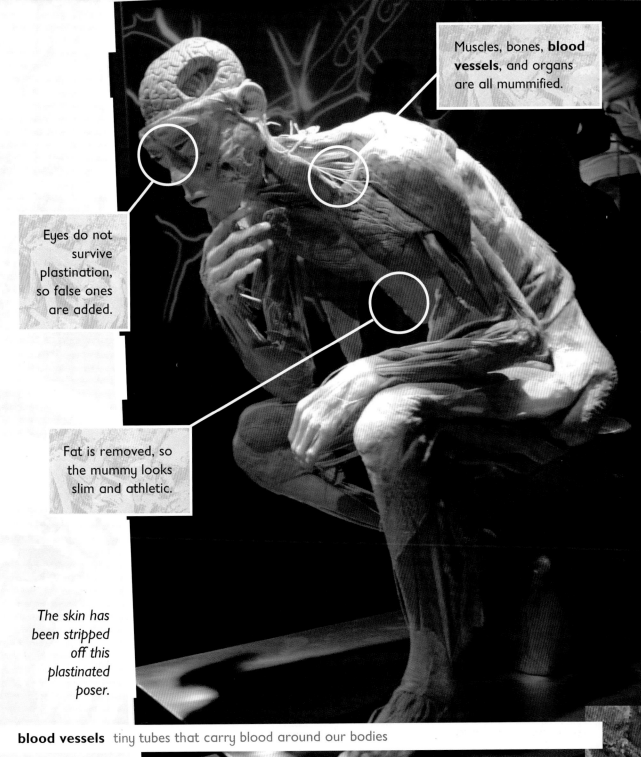

Muscles, bones, **blood vessels**, and organs are all mummified.

Eyes do not survive plastination, so false ones are added.

Fat is removed, so the mummy looks slim and athletic.

The skin has been stripped off this plastinated poser.

blood vessels tiny tubes that carry blood around our bodies

Glossary

absorb to soak up

acid substance that can cause chemical changes

adipocere name given to body fats when they turn soapy or waxy after death

afterlife life after death

airtight sealed so that air cannot get in or out

archaeologist someone who studies ancient peoples by looking at their remains

bacteria tiny cells that can both help and harm living things

blood vessels tiny tubes that carry blood around our bodies

community a group of people who live near each other

corpse a dead body

CT scanners machines that take 3-D pictures of the inside of a body

dehydrate to dry out

dissolve to break down a solid in a liquid

flint a type of stone used for old tools and weapons

intestines the tube from your stomach to your bottom

jade a valuable gemstone

manual work working with your hands, as in farming, for example

moisture wetness

organs parts of the body that do special jobs

peat mixture of rotting plants and water

philosopher someone who thinks about and studies life

pollen a powdery substance that plants use to reproduce

preserve to keep, or make last

reconstruction a copy of something that no longer survives

sacred important or holy in a particular religion

sacrificed killed as part of a religious ceremony

tomb a burial chamber

withered dried out

X-ray machines machines that take pictures of the inside of a body

Further information

Books

Mummy by James Putnam (Dorling Kindersley, 2004) A good overview of different types of mummies.

The Complete Book of Mummies by Claire Llewellyn (Wayland, 2001) Looks at how mummies—including animal mummies—are made and studied.

Mummies and Pyramids by Sam Taplin (Usbourne, 2001) Lots on Egyptian mummies as well as others—with handy internet links.

Bog Bodies: Mummies and Curious Corpses by Natalie Jane Prior (Allen and Unwin, 1996) Discover lots of different mummies made in lots of different ways.

My Best Book of Mummies by Philip Steele (Kingfisher Books, 2000) Good information on Egyptian mummies, covering all the major areas.

Web sites

FactHound offers a safe, fun way to find Internet sites related to this book. All of the sites on FactHound have been researched by our staff. Visit *www.facthound.com* for age-appropriate sites. You may browse subjects by clicking on letters, or by clicking on pictures and words. **FactHound will fetch the best sites for you!**

Films

BEWARE! Some of these films are scary!

The Curse of the Mummy's Tomb directed by Michael Carreras (Hammer, 1964) An old-fashioned horror film in which a mummy taken to England comes back to life.

The Mummy directed by Stephen Sommers (Universal, 1999) Treasure hunters accidentally awaken a 3,600-year-old Egyptian mummy, with fatal results.

The Mummy: Tomb of the Dragon Emperor directed by Rob Cohen (Universal, 2008) An action adventure. Not really about a mummy as such—more like the reawakening of a cursed Chinese Emperor.

Index